MISS FANSHAWE
AND THE
GREAT DRAGON ADVENTURE

SUE SCULLARD

M

MACMILLAN CHILDREN'S BOOKS

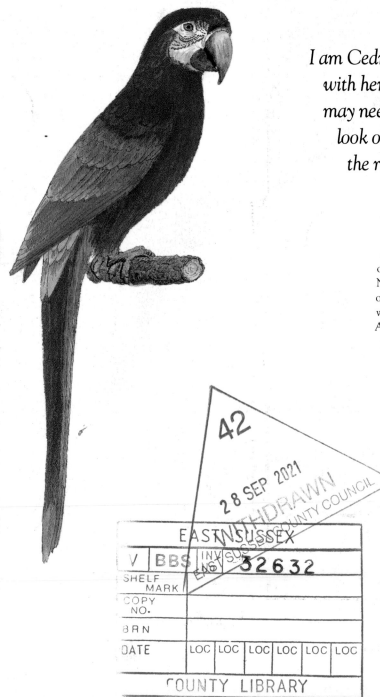

I am Cedric, Miss Fanshawe's parrot, and I go everywhere with her. As you follow her on her great adventure you may need to turn the book round. All you have to do is look out for me in the story and make sure that I'm the right way up, as I am in the picture opposite.

First published 1986 by
MACMILLAN CHILDREN'S BOOKS
A division of Macmillan Publishers Limited
London and Basingstoke
Associated companies throughout the world

Picturemac edition published 1988

British Library Cataloguing in Publication Data
Scullard, Sue
    Miss Fanshawe and the great dragon adventure.
    I. Title
823'.914[J]   PZ7

ISBN 0-333-47486-4

Typeset by Universe Typesetters Ltd.
Printed in Singapore by Imago Publishing Ltd

A long time ago there lived a great explorer called Miss Harriet Fanshawe.
She led expeditions to many remote parts of the world and brought back
strange and unusual souvenirs.

When she was little, Miss Fanshawe was not interested in dolls' houses or embroidery. She wanted adventure: to explore the tropical jungle and to climb mountains. Above all, she wanted to find a dragon.

She had always been fond of reptiles and kept two lizards and a snake in the garden shed. She watched them carefully to see if they would breathe fire.

People told her that dragons were extinct, but she would not believe them. As she grew older she became more determined than ever to prove them wrong. Not only would she find a dragon but she would bring it back to England.

Then, one day during her first expedition to Southern Patagonia, an old man told her a strange story: the centre of the earth was ruled by huge evil birds and these birds kept the lava at the earth's core red hot and molten ~ by using the fiery breath of dragons!

As she wrote the journals of her expeditions she often thought about that story. One day she would go back to Patagonia. And many years later she did.

As her ship drew near to the coast she saw smoke in the Far Mountains.

Could it be dragon smoke?

Sketches from a Journal Kept by Miss H Fanshawe.

Crossing the World's Hottest Desert
A brief sighting of the Scaly Sand Serpent
in the Burning Dunes.

Polar Expedition Day 10
Prancer with frostbitten paws.
Giant Blue Ice Lizard in crevasse.

Return to Patagonia.
A wisp of smoke in the Far Mountains.

Miss Fanshawe at once decided she must investigate. Quickly inflating the balloon with which she always travelled, she climbed into the basket and flew across to the mountains.

Near the top of the highest peak was a vast, untidy nest made of uprooted trees and branches. Inside it, snoring like thunder, was a huge reptile, curled around an egg. The reptile's breath was like hot smoke: it was a dragon.

Quickly Miss Fanshawe tied a handkerchief round her mouth, made a lasso with her rope, took out her butterfly net and cautiously approached. Deftly she got the egg into the net and the lasso over the dragon's snout. Before the dragon knew what was happening, they were away, heading for home, with the expedition's ship, the SS *Fanshawe*, keeping watch from below.

It was a long, hard journey. The Atlantic was cold and stormy, the sea birds pestered her for food and sometimes the dragon's breath made things uncomfortably warm for Miss Fanshawe.

At last they reached the shores of England and the river Thames. As they flew over Windsor Castle Miss Fanshawe thought she saw the Queen wave to her.

They landed safely in the grounds of the Tower of London.

Their arrival caused quite a stir. Everyone thought that dragons had been extinct for a long time.

The Constable of the Tower decided it would be best to put the dragon in a special cage. You couldn't be too careful with strange animals that breathed fire.

Hundreds of people came to see the dragon and her egg. Miss Fanshawe was even more famous than before. The dragon seemed pleased with all the attention she was getting and the Queen commanded a special Celebration Banquet.

It was on the day of the Banquet that the bird appeared. Miss Fanshawe was descending in her balloon when she saw the sinister creature hovering by the cage. Why was it there? What did it want?

She soon saw. The bird had stolen the egg!

Miss Fanshawe immediately changed direction and followed the bird. London and England were soon left far behind. Over seas and cold northern mountains she gave chase, until the bird ~ still holding the dragon's egg ~ slowed down and landed on the edge of a crater. Miss Fanshawe peered down ~ and the bird vanished into the darkness below.

Nothing daunted, Miss Fanshawe followed.

Return that egg at once, you wretched bird! What on earth is that down there? My goodness, it is getting rather warm.

Now where has that bird gone?
I don't like the look of that
butterfly~ I wonder where I put
my fly spray?

There's no going back now~the balloon is well and truly punctured. This heat is really stifling.

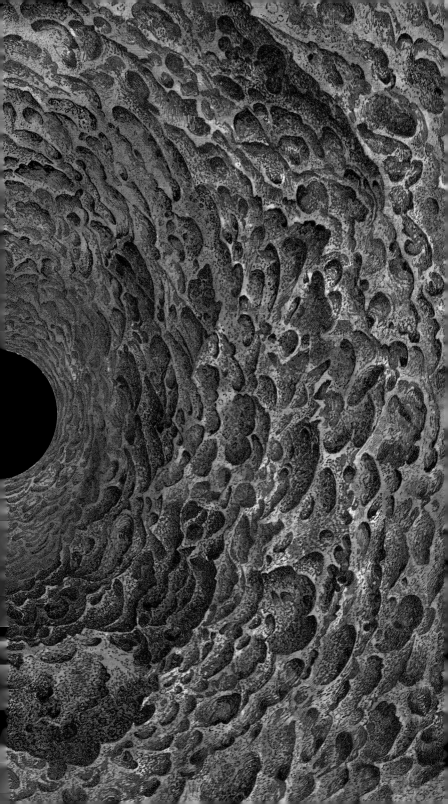

Miss Fanshawe hardly had time to take in the scene ~ dragons everywhere breathing fire on to the rocks ~ when she saw that the birds were determined to capture the young dragon. With her collapsible butterfly net she vigorously battled with her sinister attackers.

She was helped by the young dragon who caught one of the birds in his talons.
He made a noise which sounded very like "Got you!"
Could he speak as well as fly, Miss Fanshawe wondered?
Out of the corner of her eye she saw a tunnel which might be a way of escape.
But could the dragon bear her weight?

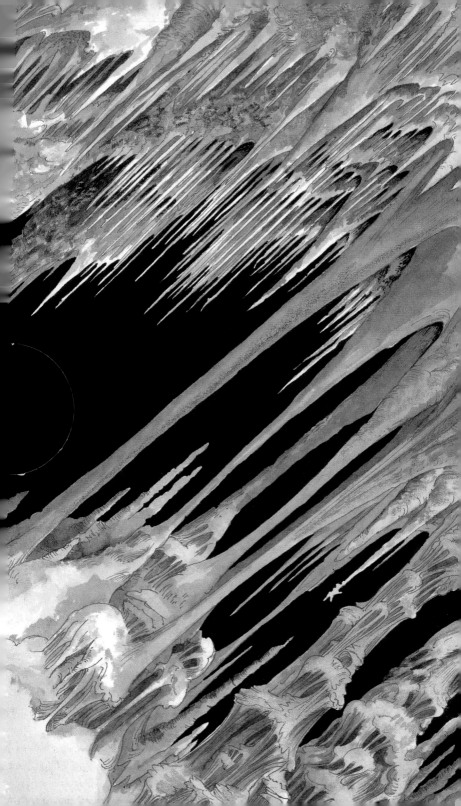

What a magnificent city! Now I can see what he was guarding. Can that be daylight up there?

I'll just burn these cobwebs and we will be out in no time.

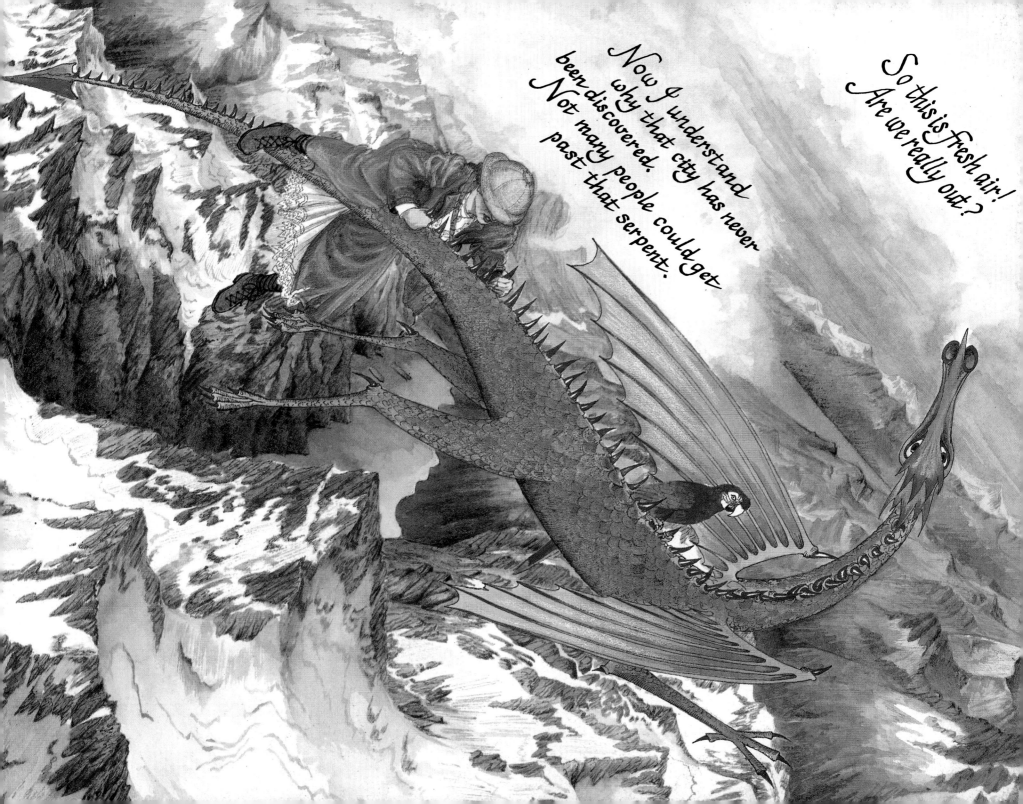

Everyone was delighted to see Miss Fanshawe back ~ and the young dragon's mother to meet her offspring for the first time.

Miss Fanshawe was tired after her journey, but she felt a good deal better after a hot bath and a nice cup of tea. She was pleased to see the dragons reunited: if it had not been for the expert flying and quick thinking of the young dragon Miss Fanshawe could not have outwitted the great serpent and escaped from the sinister birds. It could have been her Last Expedition.

The two dragons got on well together and they were always polite to the Constable of the Tower when he brought their food. They particularly enjoyed the visits of Miss Fanshawe, but they knew that what they wanted most of all was to return to the distant land of Patagonia and the Far Mountains.

Miss Fanshawe knew this too and one day she opened the door of the great cage.

As the dragons flew off on their long journey home, Miss Fanshawe waved
them farewell.
She never saw them again, but she would always remember them ~ and the
Great Dragon Adventure.